An Appreciation of Cats

a Devonshire Clinic novella by

Des DeVivo

Interior Artwork by Aethrastic Designs
Author and Cover Photography by Nicholas DeVivo
Cover Design by Des DeVivo
Cover Model: Vanya

The Library of Congress Cataloging-in-Publication Data is available upon request.

ISBN 978-1-964361-13-0 (ebook)
ISBN 978-1-964361-70-3 (paperback)

First Edition: October 2024

Book Information & Content Warnings

An Appreciation of Cats is an age gap (+20, May-December), small town, co-workers, no spice romance with melanoma awareness, older persons rep (65+), and ace rep (demi). This is the first book in a duology, but it can be read as a standalone.

This book contains: discussions of death/mortality, discussions of cancer/terminal illness, brief moments of animals in peril, detailed descriptions of physical injury and internalized homophobia.

This book is intended for readers over the age of 18.

If you discover any content you feel may need a warning that is not already listed here, please reach out to the author via email at desdevivo.writes@gmail.com or on Instagram at @desdevivo.writes

Table of Contents

To anyone who is waiting—
for love, for life, for following your dreams.
Don't let the milk spoil before you can enjoy it.

Chapter One

History

Ian

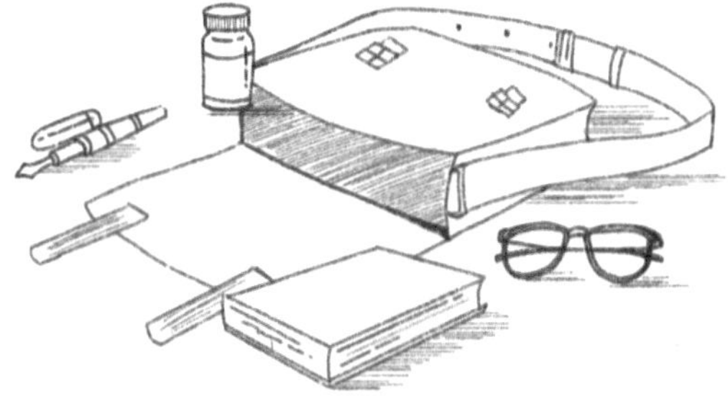

MOST PEOPLE LOOKED FORWARD to the day they were meant to retire.

Not Dr. Ian Devonshire.

In fact, that day was going to ostensibly be one of the worst of his life—for reasons that made his body toss and turn at night, that made his head whirl.

This was the only life he knew, and he'd be remiss to leave it in lieu of what came after: a quantity ill-defined. A quality even more mysterious; because *after* was, as far as he could puzzle, only the dark, gaping maw of the unknown. The cold, oppressive question of how to fill his limited remaining days with something meaningful, when for forty-three wonderful years he'd done nothing but pride himself in his position of servitude to the community at large in Holly Grove and, most prominently, the animal population of the quaint mountain town.

Aging was a rather unfortunate business, and being a veterinarian was a young man's game—a determination that, maybe even five years ago, Ian would have readily scoffed at. But he was not haughty enough to deny the truth when it came knocking on his door.

Or so he liked to believe.

Bateman purpura, they called it—diagnosing what his general practitioner saw and what Ian refused to believe when meeting the stranger who haunted his bathroom mirror. It was a generally harmless affliction in and of itself, simply the physical manifestation of what could otherwise not be so easily seen: a family history of cardiovascular disease that left him predisposed to withering blood vessels, despite a lifetime of running from the exact debilitations he presently faced. The blood thinners were a preventative measure, as were the diuretics, but

Ian found that they exacerbated his issues more than they helped. At least in the case of the immediate.

Now, his primary care doctor's orders were preventing him from efficiently and safely making determinations of his own patients, which were far less controllable than even those the local pediatrician saw: pets.

The jovial jump of an oversized mutt left his chest aching and stained with mulberry splotches.

The overexcited, nippy teeth of a puppy left his hands pocked in painful, unsightly bruises.

And the slightest snag of a scaredy cat's claw left him bleeding like a stuck pig.

The evidence was overwhelming. It was time. He was becoming a liability. And that revelation had dawned on him almost three years ago. But admitting those shortcomings came at an achingly slow pace, because to admit them to himself was to admit defeat against the hourglass.

Eventually, everyone loses; but Ian wasn't ready to.

Ready, however, was an abstract notion that fate had forced the point of when his family doctor ordered a comprehensive blood panel, and referred him to a dermatologist to confirm his diagnosis was only skin deep. The specialist, with her gentle hands and critical eyes, examined more than just the bruising on his arms, but places on his body that no one had looked at in almost three decades.

"Have you noticed any changes to this mole?" she'd asked, running her gloved fingertips over an insensitive portion of his back beneath his shoulder blade—a part of the body that was forgotten about, until it was pointed out as expressly as it was now.

"What mole?"

A seemingly innocent question that irrevocably changed everything. He'd only scheduled this appointment as a precaution of good faith and now he was being numbed for what they were assuring was a routine biopsy. Routine, perhaps for them, but unsettling for someone who hadn't considered he'd go into this office seeking a confirmation of one diagnosis, only to leave with a much deadlier one.

Apparently, most cases of skin cancer were discovered in Americans above the age of sixty-five. And apparently, British-born men who spent their days majorly under fluorescent lighting were not excluded from that statistic; especially not those of Ian's profession, who spent an inordinate amount of time being exposed to X-ray radiation.

As the dermatology technician briefed him on the aftercare of the shave biopsy they'd taken, she politely, though ignorantly, advised him to have someone at home assist him with the changing of the bandage.

And Ian had never been more aware of the deafening silence filling his home until he returned with that little paper baggy of first aid supplies with no one to hand them to.

It was then, later that night, as he sighed and grunted and twisted in front of the mirror, getting creative with a comb as a means to extend his reach, that he allowed himself to imagine what the next steps could mean. What his possibly-cancerous remaining years might look like and how he'd want to handle the indignity of them in his own, undisrupted bubble.

For even though the simple task of reapplying a bandage would've been much less of a headache with the assistance of calm and loving hands, the idea of burdening anyone—much less exposing himself in that weakness—would be an embarrassment that Ian believed far outweighed the benefit of simply asking for help. No, it was better that he keep this, like many other aspects of his personal life, close to the chest; a luxury he'd only be able to afford if he forfeited the passion of his career for the privacy of fighting for the elongation of his life, alone.

And although the truth of the matter was that his now-inevitable retirement would be a forlorn affair, Ian's only consolation was the idea that his hard-earned, self-made legacy was to be left in the good and capable hands of Dr. Alec Tarley—the man that had been his trusted assistant for the better part of a decade. A man he'd grown so very fond of.

Fond enough that he'd rather risk dislocating his own shoulder than resign to stand bare-chested in this poorly lit bathroom while his colleague applied antiseptic to his back.

Confidence in his decision rose with the morning sun and Ian dressed, cinching his tie with a sense of finality. The document had been in order for some time, because where Ian suffered in denial, he didn't in ignorance. He'd been prepared, on paper, to accept this conclusion and it was only now, with the threat of total incapacity looming over him, that he dug the envelope from his filing cabinet and tucked it into his bag.

For the town being so small, the practice was always busy. This was partially because the number of cats, dogs, hamsters, and horses far outweighed the number of human residents in Holly Grove. Not to mention their proximity to the other tiny towns of neighboring altitudes who weren't lucky enough to have their own veterinary practices established conveniently in the town square.

It also helped that Holly Grove's mayor was a golden retriever aptly named Grover (the third) and that Devonshire Clinic was the mayor's exclusive provider of nail trimmings and flea medication. Having the mayor's endorsement was vital, and the front desk assistant capitalized on that by designing cheeky 'seals of approval', then taping them to the shop's front window. *If It's Good Enough For Grover!*

The echoing slam of the Vauxhall's door was carried on the mist of the autumn morning air as Ian shouldered on his leather satchel. It was an ancient thing, part briefcase, part messenger bag of personal items that got him through the long workdays. Trinkets like a spare pair of spectacles, a just-in-case mass-market paperback for the all-elusive quiet moment, a fountain pen, his lunch of egg salad sandwich, and a half-empty bottle of Advil.

Like the fiery leaves that littered the damp asphalt, his eyes danced across the parking lot, taking stock in vehicles both known and foreign to him. Though none stood out as readily as the presence of an emerald green Land Rover, which prompted the unconscious upward tick of the edges of his lips as he imagined the face of the man who owned it.

Careful not to let his bag's strap rub the sensitive spot freshly carved under his shoulder, Ian pulled open the rear door of his practice and ducked into his personal office to deposit his bag and overcoat. Crossing the darkened room, Ian tended to the blinds on the windows, letting in ample light; and although he would've rather conducted this private business in the covert of shadows, his eyesight wasn't what it used to be. From the crack in the open door, he could already hear the genial chatter of boarded dogs anxious for their morning meals, a ringing phone quickly answered, and the lobby bell's jingle as the first of their patients were walked through the front door. As his ears stayed tuned to the hallway, Ian stowed the envelope from his satchel into the top drawer of his desk—one hiding place closer to a revelation.

Slowly, Ian sealed the drawer before fixing his expression to one that he hoped most resembled one that he wore on any other Monday, wherein the presence of life-altering news wasn't weighing big, purple bags under his eyes. Leaving the sanctity of his office behind, he paced the brightly lit hallway to the front desk where their resident slice-of-sunshine was waiting to greet not just the public, but the staff.

"Mornin', Dr. Devonshire." Connie smiled over her shoulder.

"Good morning, Connie. What's on?"

Connie spun around in her desk chair and handed the Doctor a clipboard, which featured a printout of the day's patient schedule. His eyes flickered over the page, and, like clockwork, his heart ached at the audacity of the owners and the poor, prideful pets that had to answer to such blasphemous names the likes of Ashes, Pinkerton, and Mr. Squeaks-A-Lot.

However, nothing affected his heart more than scanning the list and seeing the name of his always-assigned attendant. Theirs would be the hardest appointment he'd keep that day.

"Tarley's already in exam one," Connie said, gesturing with a peony-painted finger.

"Oh, is he now?"

"You know him," she laughed.

And Ian smiled, because, most fortunately, he did.

Chapter Two

Normalcy

Alec

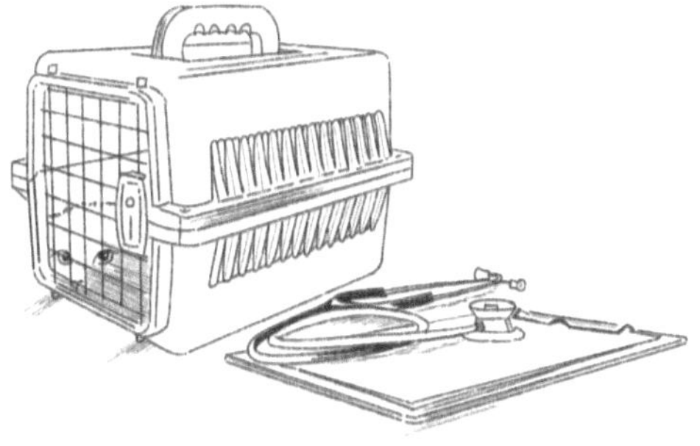

Two raps at the door, not subtle or sweet.

A brief pause, the length of a heartbeat.

The twist of a brass knob.

The squeak of worn leather shoes on robin's egg-colored, slip-resistant vinyl flooring.

"Tarley."

His heart fluttered.

And that's exactly how it'd gone for the last eight years.

Transplanting himself in this small town had been an unexpected decision, even if it was one that he'd spent his whole life working towards. The city, with its pretty lights and ease of convenience, was perfect for a past version of himself: a younger, more bright-eyed man who sought nothing but the thrill of difference, sprinkled with nights of intrigue.

When Alec Tarley first moved to Los Angeles, he'd been little more than a kid, with the goalposts of his dreams set no further than what his dazzled mind could conceive or what his ignorance-stunted fingers could reach for.

He hadn't always been a veterinarian. Before that he'd been nothing more than a handsome face perfect for stock images, toothpaste ads, and embodying the nameless people populating the backgrounds of car insurance commercials. Something about the work had, in the beginning, felt redeeming—as if a man from the middle of nowhere could go somewhere. Be someone.

But time quickly eroded the glitter of those cinema lights until the LEDs revealed something grim and honestly quite ugly. He'd been fooled. What he'd thought had been giving him purpose had only been giving him short-term doses of dopamine; and though the monetary payout of each job was sufficient, the jobs themselves, as he aged, became far and few between.

Without ever realizing or anticipating it, his prime had come and gone before he reached thirty; and while there was certainly a market for 'refined looking men' who were prematurely graying, he had the salt-and-pepper temples without the sculpted jaw, which automatically marked him as noncompliant. Unwanted. Unneeded.

Until the rare, rainy evening when a very pregnant cat waddled up to his apartment door.

After that, the purpose of his existence just seemed obvious, like fate had taken him by the hand and shown him the way to a life he was better suited for.

The cat's miserable mewlings were accurately interpreted, and Alec, thinking quickly, brought the flea-infested stray inside. The delivery was complicated only by the fact that the mother was inexperienced, and the kittens had become increasingly entangled in their own umbilical cords, to the point that one stopped moving. Alec jumped into action, and with steady hands, gently freed the biological fiber wrapped about their tiny legs and necks until blood was smeared up to his wrists—but everyone was alive, and happily nursing.

From her prone position, the exhausted mother lifted her gaze up to him, and Alec could not only physically feel an extended aura of gratitude, but plainly see it reflected in the animal's eyes.

No one else on the planet had ever made him feel like that before. Like his presence actually mattered. Like *he* had actually made a difference.

Shortly thereafter, Alec enrolled in his first courses of veterinary education. And even though the decision felt haphazard and he, himself, just plain late to the game, Alec came to realize that there never truly was such a thing as poor timing: only the troubling realization of an opportunity missed.

A mistake that Alec Tarley would be remiss to ever make again.

Thus, even after graduating in the top of his class, securing a doctoral position at a well-established chain of veterinary hospitals, and actively living a fulfilling life that he once only dreamed of, Alec found himself still plagued with a gnawing sense of despondency. One that he couldn't simply ignore. He picked and prodded the feeling until he uncovered within himself its root: that the lifestyle his soul came to yearn for was clashing with the one he'd carved out. His adult body craved the familiarity of his youth. For wide-open spaces not filled in with concrete; for clean air, friendly neighbors, and most of all, the color green.

Stability was now the end game.

That, and peace.

So, Alec began casting hooks into the deep end, keeping shallow expectations; shocked by the pressure applied to his line when, swifter than he'd anticipated, he got a bite.

His query had been answered.

His application, not only reviewed, but accepted.

An interview set. An offer extended.

"I believe you'll make a great addition to the team," the Doctor and owner of the veterinary practice had commended in an alluring British accent, made tinny from the sequestered town's poor reception. And those were the only words Alec needed to begin the process of packing up his studio apartment to move into a cheaper, yet roomier, two-bedroom cabin, four thousand feet above sea level in California's Santa Rosa Mountain Range.

What he'd wanted at twenty-five wasn't what he wanted at thirty-five.

Or forty-five, for that matter.

And especially now that he was staring down the barrel of his rapidly approaching fifties, Alec couldn't help but take what he'd learned through those decades and re-evaluate the winds of his own inevitable change. Which felt like an odd restlessness to relent to, because as much as Alec was content with his current state of being, an unsatisfied part of him yearned to reach for something more.

For someone more.

"Hey, Doc." Alec beamed, as he whirled around from where he was polishing the exam table with a disinfectant wipe. The room, which smelt of latex and lemon, was instantly infiltrated by the duskier scent of cloves and clementine; a scent he'd not only come to expect but to crave.

Ian closed the exam room door behind him and crossed his arms tight across his chest.

"Hm?" Alec prompted the Doctor, stepping on the pedal of a trash can to pop open the lid and dispose of the wipe.

"How many times must I remind you, you don't have to do that?"

"Do what?"

Ian gestured to the sparkling, stainless steel tabletop. "That."

Alec shrugged. "I like doing that."

"What? Getting under my skin?"

"No...Preparing the room for you."

For us.

Ian's gaze tipped over his glasses, and Alec met his pensive stare, wondering just how long Ian would have to pin him to the spot for him to admit the words he meant to say out loud, but hadn't.

Then Ian's tight-lipped mouth softened into a smirk; and it was moments like these that Alec felt reassured he wasn't the only one suffering with the isolation of internalizations not expressed to even his closest colleague. Something about the stubbornness of Ian's refusal to release him scratched an itch Alec had been chasing: to not simply be looked at, but also seen.

A sudden, though polite, knock at the door caused Alec's eyes to be the first to swing away as he swallowed down phrases gone too long unspoken. Wondering where his courage had fled to. Wondering why he'd become a stranger to the *him* that had once promised not to tiptoe around opportunity like a ticking time bomb, but to seize it readily, lest die trying.

Despite how small Holly Grove was, Alec didn't require a full hand to count the times that they'd crossed each other's paths outside the clinic. They'd encountered each other only twice in eight years. Once, at the market, when Ian had been purchasing bundles of wood prior to a snowstorm. Alec had approached him, then—or rather, had startled him. And because of how awkwardly flustered Ian had seemed at the intrusion and how awkwardly flustered Alec became as a result, the second time he'd seen Ian in public, Alec had been too apprehensive to make himself known. Instead, he'd kept his distance, watching the Doctor from afar, wondering what it might be like to sit across from him at the diner's sticky Formica tabletop as something more than a colleague...or more than a friend.

It was just that when those olive eyes found him across the span of disinfected spaces, Alec could only recall the fuzzy feeling of being wanted, then becoming crippled by the fear of what change might invite to the quality of their easy camaraderie. Ultimately, Alec knew he'd rather cherish what they had now, than risk losing it altogether by reaching for grasses that only seemed greener from the other side.

"Ah, yes, do come in," Ian said to the door, after clearing his throat and smoothing the front of his lab coat.

As expected, it was Connie who peeked in and passed a clipboard into Alec's awaiting hands. He'd snapped back to dutiful attention when the crackling air was effectively doused by Connie's interruption. "Mrs. Jones," Connie announced, though Alec wasn't sure if she was referencing the woman plodding into the room or whomever it was she had in the carrier.

Genial as usual, especially around familiar faces, Ian's eyes lit up. "Mrs. Jones! Why, it's been so long. How have you been getting on?" he asked, meeting the homely woman halfway across the tiny room and greeting her fondly before guiding her to set the carrier on the exam table. While they caught up, Alec took his practical role as Ian's shadow, slotting into the corner to peer just over the man's right shoulder.

"I know, I know. I've missed her last two appointments—"

"Four," Alec corrected, with a quick glance at the paperwork. This interjection earned him an unfavorable look from the Doctor, which wasn't so much an actual look as it was an unnatural silence, where Ian became so still that not even the sound of his clothes shifting as he breathed was perceptible.

Where on the other hand, Mrs. Jones barely seemed to register Alec's observation, as she absentmindedly asked, "Oh, was it really?" and continued to creak open the rusted springs on the carrier door.

In an effort to remedy his faux pas, Alec sat the clipboard aside and gestured to Mrs. Jones. "Allow me?" he offered, as pathetic sounds of a clawed resistance resonated from within the hard-shell container.

"That's alright, I'll get her," Mrs. Jones said. "She's not good with strangers."

Alec took the dismissal as a cue and stepped back, albeit with reluctance. Ian's energy had ebbed into something soothing and forgiving, granting Alec the permission he needed to stand down.

After some effort, Mrs. Jones scooped out what looked to be a half-melted puddle of Rocky Road ice cream. Alec shot a curious glance at Ian as the woman cooed into the bundle of bedraggled fur in her arms. It was only then, cuddled close against her owner's breast, that terrified eyes turned out to the room where awaiting men in white coats were introduced to a feline face with the most magnificent clover-colored eyes.

"Awh!" Alec melted, and beside him, Ian smiled.

"There she is." Ian motioned to the table. "Come, now, Patches. Let's have a nice long look at you."

Mrs. Jones sat Patches down on the cool, reflective tabletop, and Ian stepped flush to the table's edge, carrying on in his usual conversational way as pale fingers stroked investigatively over the shivering cat's head, neck, and shoulders. The feline hunched, furry feet sliding on the steel as it attempted to crouch and instead splayed, reducing further.

"What seems to be the trouble, Mrs. Jones?" Ian asked.

"Well, nothing really, I just wanted to…"

The conversation in the room filtered away when Alec, half-turned, collecting vials of vaccines, was stalled by the realization that the whites of Patches' eyes had become stark, her pupils dilated into black pits. The cat cast an anxious gaze back at Ian's hands palpitating her sides, and Alec's heart dropped.

"Uh, Doc—"

But it was too late.

Alec watched helplessly as irritation bolted through the cat's expression like lightning, severing its patience and activating its instincts. Patches was wired to fight, not take flight. The cat twisted, moving at a startling speed and striking with a disturbing accuracy—her claws strumming across the chorded tendons stretching the top of Ian's hand.

The Doctor recoiled from the hiss of bared teeth and stepped back into Alec, who pressed a steadying hand against the older man's lower back.

"Ah! Quick little bugger," Ian muttered and shuffled around Alec to flick on the tap of the inset sink, letting the cold water wash over the jagged tears. The water ran pink.

To ensure that Patches didn't attempt to scrabble off the table, Alec barred his forearms around her fluff. Patches simply licked her mouth and shivered somehow lower.

"Oh no! Dr. Devonshire!" Mrs. Jones gasped. "I'm so sorry, I—"

"No, no. It's no trouble at all," Ian rushed to assure. "Simply a hazard of the job."

From here, Alec could see that Patches' latest nail trim must have been at her last appointment—though he didn't make anything more than a mental note. Instead, he stroked two fingers along the top of her triangular head and glanced over his shoulder at where Ian was now dab-drying his hand and using the paper towel to apply pressure to the readily bleeding wound.

Although Mrs. Jones took Ian's dismissal for face value, the Doctor's pursed lips spoke louder than any words. The man's profound distaste for either his failing agility or his skin's traitorous fragility was clearer to Alec than even the spice of copper tingeing the air. A fat droplet of blood hit the floor with a smack, and Ian exhaled a smile before tearing off another paper towel and adding it to his failing attempt at triage.

"You'll have to excuse me, Mrs. Jones," Ian said, gesturing slightly with his preoccupied hands. "But don't you worry. Patches is in perfectly good hands with Dr. Tarley."

The phrase made blood rush simultaneously to and from his head as Alec both blanched and blushed in a shocking tandem that left him dizzy.

"Isn't that right?" Ian asked.

Alec was forced to meet Ian's gaze, and the Doctor tilted his head almost fondly at the image of his assistant taming the shrew, while Alec's fingers scratched the poof of Patches' chin and rumbles of contentment vibrated in the feline's chest.

"Perfectly," Alec replied.

Ian flashed a smile at Mrs. Jones and gave a short, respectful nod before snagging the handle of the door leading to the back hallways and treatment areas, disappearing. The little trail of bloody droplets that followed him out was the only evidence that remained, beyond the lingering smell of his cologne. Alec paused for a fortifying breath before returning his gaze to the pallid-looking owner, then to her equally disarrayed pet. Then, he calmly removed the stethoscope from around his neck.

"Apologies, Mrs. Jones. Now...you were saying?"

Chapter Three

The Proposal

Ian

EVENTUALLY THE BLEEDING STOPPED and normalcy resumed, as it most always did after tragedy. Slow at first, then steady, until the scar of that tear in reality was nothing but a faint imperfection that few remembered.

However, each of these seemingly minuscule blunders felt like monoliths to Ian. A skyscraper-sized domino crashing down, backing him to the edge of a cliff he'd soon be made to jump from. Except, today he'd come prepared with a plan to take control of the situation before it got to the point where his hand was forced, and his ability to approach the situation with a clear head was forfeited.

Or so he'd desired the case to be, even though his courage wavered, contrary to that former conviction.

The burble of the electric kettle mimicked his nerves, jostling into one another in a frantic jumble just beneath the surface of his thinning skin. It was almost time for their usual appointment of midday reprieve, and the subtle sound of well-known soles scuffing down the clinic's hallway caused both hope and despair to swell within him. This was the moment Ian had been both waiting for and equally dreading; and the fact that it was here—that *he* was here—made the script that Ian had perfected vanish entirely from his mind.

Three raps at the office door, gentle but eager, alerted Ian to his intended guest. The sound, along with the promise of what was to follow it, made the edges of his mouth curl instinctively into a coy smile of subdued pleasure. Ian would be hard-pressed to let on regarding his true feelings surrounding the man who had been working for him for the last near-decade. Though, Ian was suddenly far less concerned about keeping that secret when he had another, far more pressing one weighing on his mind.

Ian's eyes flicked to the clock hanging on the wall. It was four p.m. on the dot.

"Come in."

The door creaked open. "Hey, Doc." And Tarley slipped inside.

The office was small but sufficient. Ian's credentials were proudly hung on the cream-colored walls, as were a selection of thank-you notes, photographs, and crayon drawings from the owners of his patients. A heavy mahogany desk sat at the back, headed by an uncomfortable office chair. Up front were two faded, floral wingback chairs with a sturdy side table stationed between them. A low, long filing cabinet sat against the side wall—the perfect makeshift worktop for a modest selection of biscuit boxes, tea tins, and the boiling kettle. Tarley quietly closed the door and shrugged off his fur-mottled, white lab coat. He hung it on a standing coatrack, alongside Ian's own, then stepped in close to Ian's elbow to oversee the process of plating their selection of desserts. Or so, Ian assumed.

"How's that hand?"

The compassion with which Tarley visually assessed the wrap of his wound prompted Ian to dream of how his assistant might otherwise care for the one on his back if only he knew of its existence. Or how a man like Tarley might assuage his fears as he sat connected to an IV drip of life-saving liquid in the race against malignancy and the somewhat frivolous pursuit of ringing a bell.

No. He refused to let his mind wander to the improbable—for while he was certainly the type of man to preemptively plan the crossing of bridges yet discovered, he couldn't allow himself to hope Tarley would care to join him on such an arduous, final journey.

"Fine."

"It's bled through."

Ian glanced down at the small, burgundy stain marring the beige bandage and hummed consideringly. He paused only a moment to make this assessment before continuing to pour water over the loose-leaf black tea in the infuser of the ceramic serving pot. "Only enough that changing it would do little more than disrupt the clotting."

"And what of keeping up appearances?"

"...What of them?" Ian averted his gaze before expertly turning about-face, balancing the silver tray of china and landing it on the table set between the chairs. Behind him, Tarley gave a meted sigh, then picked up a pre-set plate of biscuits. Ian settled into his seat, impatient for the tea to steep, as Tarley plopped into the adjoining chair and snagged a Jaffa Cake, before offering the plate out for Ian to make his usual selection of Biscoff. Tarley sat the plate aside and both men stewed in contemplation of their biscuits and all thoughts adjacent, though none nearly as sweet. Instead of taking a precursory bite, Tarley sat his biscuit aside.

"Y'know, I wish you wouldn't call me that."

Ian's heart stuttered—not a good or common thing for a man of his age—but he accepted the discomfort for the opportunity it gave to take hold of Tarley's gaze and keep it for a prolonged, probing period of time. "I...beg your pardon?"

"Doctor," Alec replied, lips tight, though his gaze faltered briefly. And as the silence that stretched between them became apparently too much for the young man to stomach, Alec piqued again, leaning forward in his chair. "Your first patient this morning."

Our, Ian corrected, though he did not voice it.

His silence prompted Tarley to clarify. "You called me Doctor."

"Oh. Yes. Well—"

"Well, I really wish you wouldn't."

It was a tiresome game they played, moving titles like chess pieces. Tarley hadn't lost his veterinary credentials and years of experience earning them just because he'd accepted this fabricated position of 'assistant.' However, Tarley had a habit of honoring the denomination too highly for Ian's tastes, and reinforced it vehemently, no matter how often Ian tried to equate their positions.

Ian itched with the anticipation of a known answer. Still he asked, "And why's that?"

"Because I'm not a doctor."

"But you are, Tarley." Ian huffed, discarding his own uneaten biscuit and wiping the crumbs from his fingers, decidedly. "In every manner but title."

Aside from having been completely infatuated with the easygoing nature of the man on the other end of the telephone, Ian had convinced himself that his innate desire to hire Alec Tarley, despite his gross over-qualifications, had been completely benign. It was just good business, he'd told himself, to employ a man of such high caliber. Tarley's reasoning for wanting to accept the position, although it was of lower pay and station than his prior employment in the city, was entirely his own. Ian had never interrogated him on that. And although Ian had been enthralled with the idea of meeting Tarley in person, he then, perhaps quite selfishly, was inclined to keep him once he'd gotten a taste of how easily they got on.

The irony surrounding the fact that *he* was now the one with the intention of leaving wasn't lost on him; in fact, it was quite the painful pill to swallow—much less keep down. Ian creaked up from his chair.

"That's exactly my point," Tarley returned, gaze tracking Ian on his trail behind his desk. Tarley's head tilted with curiosity as he reminded Ian, "I'm your assistant."

It took every ounce of control remaining in Ian's feeble body not to debilitate Tarley with a scoff. Instead, Ian swallowed his heartache and delved a hand into the top drawer of his desk to withdraw the envelope tucked inside as he smiled weakly and said, "Of that, I'm well aware."

Their eyes met and the room simmered, not so unlike the leaves left steeping in the pot.

"It has been the highlight of my days for quite some time now," Ian admitted.

Tarley's throat wavered with a hard swallow, and his tongue flickered out to wet his lips for a timid utterance. "You...say that like there's a reason it can't continue."

Tarley's gaze fell to the ominous envelope as Ian rounded his desk and approached. He extended the letter, encouraging Tarley to take it, but he made no such effort. Instead, Tarley simply lifted his eyes, peering through his lashes with a brightened hopefulness that made Ian's chest ache. "What's this?"

"A proposal," Ian said.

"...Of partnership?"

"No. Of ownership."

Tarley shook his head slowly, not understanding what, for Ian, was tortuously clear. He hadn't wanted to say it, using so many words. But Tarley was either being intentionally thick or was allowing denial to blind him to the obvious.

"I'm retiring."

Then, shockingly, Tarley's despondency broke with a laugh—one that filtered away when Ian didn't crack a smile. "You can't be serious."

"I am."

"When?"

Ian paused, delaying the admittance. "Soon."

Of all the reactions Ian had prepared himself for, the dejection evident on Tarley's stricken face hadn't been among them.

"...How soon is *soon*?"

Ian gestured slightly with the envelope. "However soon you sign."

Still, Tarley refused to take the letter. He looked at it, and Ian's injured hand, as if they were something crawled straight from a nightmare; a haunting vision that Ian was able to see, too, the longer he stared at the evidence of the proposition he'd just made. One that had, sorely, gone unaccepted.

Instead of forcing the point, Ian tucked the envelope under the plate of biscuits near Tarley's side of the table and distracted himself from the thrum of discouraged silence that wound itself in the distance between them. Only the soft tinkle of tea being poured broke the quiet while Tarley focused on a particularly interesting speck on the floor, as if damming the forward momentum of this conversation would void its continuation, altogether. However, this revelation would not be so easily swept under the rug now that it had been discovered—much as the biopsy on which Ian was anxiously awaiting the results of.

"I realize that this is quite a lot of information to take in..." Ian offered quietly, as he plunked a cube of sugar into each cup, along with a splash of milk. With slow, conscientious swirls of a small spoon, Ian mixed Tarley's tea, then his own, as he mused aloud, "Perhaps I ought to have anticipated your hesitancy, but I thought you'd be happy for me, and more importantly, for yourself."

Ian lifted the teacup on its saucer and extended it to Tarley, whose gaze stuttered up from the floor to meet Ian's. Their fingers grazed as Tarley accepted the tea, but the rhythmic clink of the ceramic betrayed Tarley's usually sure hands, and he took the teacup by the handle to silence the treachery of his splintering resolve.

"It's just...I...I'm not ready."

Ian smiled, head tipping. His knees felt weak—his heart too—but instead of wallowing in the growing grief of a future amputation, Ian attempted to assure them both that this was the right decision, by telling one truth and then a lie.

"But you *are* ready for this, Tarley. And so am I."

Chapter Four

Digesting The News
Alec

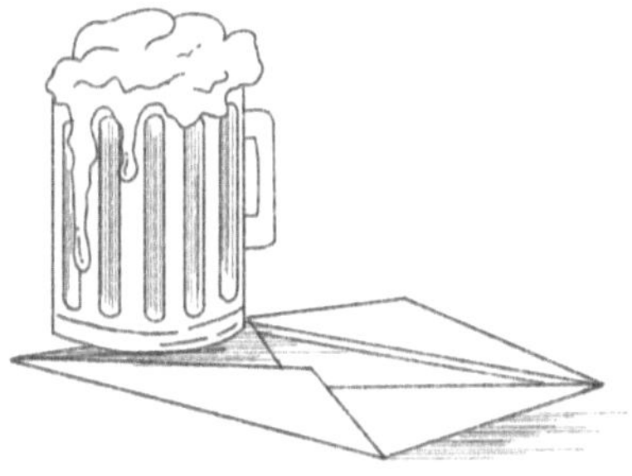

TIME OFTEN FORGOT LITTLE towns like Holly Grove.

Which was why, against all odds and ordinances, Alec found himself wrapped in a hug of cigarette smoke that was no better at comforting him than the warmth of the alcohol flowing through his veins. The downers introduced by the frosty beers upon which he sipped warred with the uppers introduced by the secondhand hits of nicotine, but Alec was certain that neither sensation was the cause of the nausea currently plaguing every vital organ between his head and his heart.

The need to run was dulled by his instinct to hide—and so Alec sat in the bar's hazy darkness, with the arch of his sneaker stirruped on the rung of his stool. His knee bounded as if half of his soul were sprinting a marathon, and his back bent as if the other half were priming to take a nap right there on the bar.

Alec raised his glass, expecting to take a refreshing swallow, but his mouth met nothing but foam. The bubbles kissed his upper lip and left it coated in a smeary mustache. Apparently, the barkeep noticed him attempting to drink from an empty mug because he quirked a brow and asked, "Another?"

"Oh. Um." Alec was quick to use the denim sleeve of his coat to wipe his mouth free of the offense. He looked down into the suds, which fizzled and popped, dying before his eyes.

Alec hadn't meant to come here, hadn't meant to be on his now-third beer of the night when he'd then need to sober up enough to drive home. And yet, somehow, it was exactly what he'd been aiming for, without having any malicious intent. Some things just happen like that, leading to both good and bad decisions. The same way Alec knew that sometimes, such decisions could be both good and bad, simultaneously.

It would not be wise to accept the barkeep's proposition—a thought which struck him harder, knowing the full weight of the envelope which sat as heavy as a brick in his pocket—an equally daunting offer he would be as foolish to accept as the beer he then permissed. "Yeah."

This won Alec a skeptical look, but the barkeep gathered the empty mug and tromped over to the spigots of the kegs mounted on the back wall. He thrust the empty glass under the tap and pulled the lever, splashing fresh drink into Alec's leftover backwash. "Don't remember seein' you 'round here before," the barkeep said, turning squinted eyes at him.

Alec shied from the gaze, giving a diffident shrug of his shoulder, the stubble of his cheek scraping against the sheepskin collar of his jacket. "Yeah, well..."

"He's the guy's gonna take over for ole Devonshire," a slumped figure sitting smack dab in the middle of the bar muttered. A cigarette smoldered between his fingers and smoke puffed from his lips with each pronunciation as he continued with an indicative hike of his thumb. "When he finally retires."

Alec's stomach turned. Although the benefits of this rural lifestyle far outweighed those of city living, Alec had forgotten this particular downside of being a resident in such a small town: word had a tendency to spread worse than wildfire. And while Alec couldn't be sure if this man knew of Ian Devonshire's fact or if his comment was based solely on speculation, the stranger's intuition made every hair stand to attention on the back of Alec's neck. He was struck by a troubling sense of exposure, a vulnerability borne of the self-awareness of one's own perceived nakedness—though there was absolutely no way this man could have actual knowledge of what Alec kept in his pocket.

The barkeep huffed, snapping off the tap and letting the foam flow over the sides of the glass as he evened out the pour. He nodded over to Alec. "That you?"

"...I work with Dr. Devonshire, yes."

Alec became hyper-aware of his unconscious choice of using the word *with*, instead of *for*. Neither man seemed to notice. His beer was sloshed down on the countertop, and Alec glanced up to the bartender's reddish face glowering down at him with a grin a touch too curly to be anything but teasing. "This a celebration, then?"

Alec's gaze ticked between the men before he snared the mug's cold handle and shifted off the stool.

"No."

The firmness with which he dispelled their inquiry existed contrary to the disruption raging inside. Ian had asked him to find the positive in a proposal that he could only manage to view as a negative, and his inability to achieve what Ian asked of him left him aching with the barbed guilt of his failure.

Taking his replenished drink, Alec distanced himself from the company at the bar by finding a high-top table in a secluded corner. Waylon Jennings played from the jukebox's crackling speakers, and here in the shadows, Alec felt as isolated as he could be from the prying eyes of Holly Grove's townspeople. It occurred to him, as he reached into the discreet inner breast pocket of his coat to drag his finger over the envelope's outer folds, that perhaps he should have taken this pity party back to the privacy of his cabin. However, Alec didn't truly want to be alone right now, even if he also didn't want to be hovered over and actively confronted with his grief.

Although he'd ultimately taken Ian's letter, he hadn't opened it. The remainder of their afternoon tea went without further discussion of Ian's decision. And while Alec tried his best to appear unaffected by the knowledge, Ian bested him at greeting their remaining patients with a smile that understated the destruction of the bomb he'd recently dropped—except Alec knew that Ian wasn't unscathed, no matter how well he tried to mask his heart's affliction.

Alec hadn't been able to shake the look in Ian's eye when he'd handed over the envelope as if he were severing off a piece of himself in offering. Alec had always been cursed with the uncanny ability to read eyes, and while Ian's face had been stony, if not sorrowful in its expression, his eyes had been a forest of information of hard tidings and fear and pain.

But why?

It didn't make any sense. Why now, of all times, was Ian making this call?

What was the rush?

Sure, his health had been stumbling—that was no big secret—but it hadn't *failed*. Everyone at the clinic had survived their fair shares of bumps, scratches, hell, even bites. That was, as Ian always said, just a hazard of the job. But this, whatever Ian dealt with, was somehow *personal*.

After taking a sip of his drink, Alec fished the envelope from his pocket. He examined it for a moment. His name hand-written on the front, the practice's logo in the upper corner. He tore open the envelope and pulled out the letter. It was a one-page contract. Nothing flowery. Just a black-and-white version of what Ian had already expressed: that upon the TBD date of his retirement, Ian Devonshire would promote Alec Tarley to head veterinarian, transferring his patients and relinquishing complete ownership of the practice.

Oh, Doc. What're you doing? Alec thought with a sigh.

Doc. A moniker that would disintegrate with Ian's title. But that wouldn't be all Alec would be forced to lose if he assumed the role that Ian was all but begging him to take.

Except Ian's position wasn't a prize to be won—it was superfluous to what, or rather who, Alec actually wanted. Because while signing the offer would certainly solidify his career and his life here in Holly Grove, accepting the offer also meant that he'd be solidifying the singular absence which his heart would suffer the most.

It wasn't fair.

Wasn't fair for Ian to assume that Alec would accept, much less actually *want* this change, this separation. Just as it wasn't fair for Alec to assert control, to deny Ian his retirement, like Ian belonged to him in any meaningful way outside the title 'esteemed colleague'. They didn't own one another any more than they *owed* one another—which was partially why this extension of absolute faith, this gift, was upsetting to Alec in so many ways.

What had he actually done to deserve the inheritance of his mentor's life's work?

Mentor. A word that had been privately assigned and considered without ever having been known by the other party in this exchange. Although their relationship, as it currently stood, had strengthened throughout the years, it was Alec who bolstered it into unfamiliar places without Ian's consent or knowledge.

In layman's terms, Alec had never told Ian that he loved him.

The timing had never felt right, the connection they shared too fragile or the moment too fleeting, and now...

Well, now it was too late.

By signing this document, he'd be dooming them both to a life of solitude. A life that, though Ian never expressed it, Alec knew neither truly wanted. So, the question remained, nagging and burning at the back of his mind: of all the times, of all the avenues of exit...

Why this? Why now?

And of any man on Earth eligible for this honor, why *him*?

Chapter Five

Distances and Whys

Ian

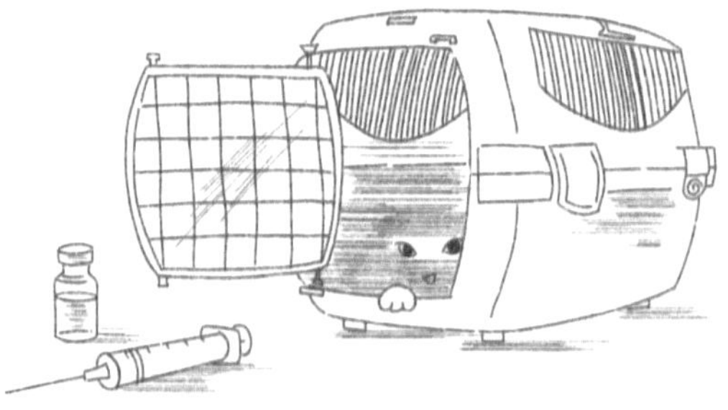

IT WAS EASIER TO lie to himself than it was to lie to Tarley.

In the uncomfortable comfort of his own space, in the familiarity of the house's most lonely shadows, Ian could sit in his threadbare chair and pretend that he had all the answers.

He could forget that he needed to change a bandage that he couldn't properly reach.

He could forget the discouraging results of the biopsy that were now being sent away for a second opinion.

And he could forget that he'd officially decided on his retirement prior to obtaining Tarley's consent.

Days had been draining away without the answers Ian required to make an informed decision. He was losing control, and in an attempt to retain hold of the reins, Ian had made the foolhardy decision to take Tarley's agency away. An action that he justified by allowing the anxiety he felt to turn into resentment—failing to realize that no one could ever understand him, or his decision, if he never gave them the opportunity to.

Yes, by far, it was easier to lie to himself than it was to lie to Alec Tarley—so Ian undermined him, then pushed him away.

A nasty habit that was becoming an unfortunate track record.

Over the years, Ian had learned to better balance his occupational obsession. And while he'd always been stubborn to step away—filling his weekdays with appointments and his weekends with house calls—meeting Tarley had complicated things, dredging up desires he hadn't felt for anyone in decades. Because eight years ago, when Tarley joined the practice, Ian began to find his inclination to spend time at his facility evolving from a want to a stringent need.

One he indulged in.

A connection he fostered, perhaps a little too much—because years ago, when Tarley had first inquired about seeing Ian for tea outside of clinic hours in the privacy of a home, Ian blanched...torn between appeasing his own selfishness and keeping up appearances.

Ian couldn't be certain that the reputation he'd built for himself in this little community could withstand the weight of a scandal. Whatever concern he held for Holly Grove's ability to stomach his own sexuality was eclipsed by his concern of how a relationship with his underling might be perceived. Ian loathed the idea that Tarley's merit as his assistant—or as his successor—would be questioned as a result of any romantic connection they shared.

Not that Ian was certain that Tarley's proposal was one of courtship—but it didn't matter. For Ian, it wouldn't do. Even if Tarley *was* asking him around for tea as a means of pursuing fledgling feelings, Tarley deserved more than this; more than what someone twenty years his senior could offer in terms of spunk and longevity.

Tarley deserved more than stolen glances and cups of tea shared behind locked doors.

"It wouldn't be proper, I'm afraid," Ian had answered, after a stumbling recovery of his resolve. An answer that haunted him. He'd drawn a line in concrete too quick-drying to retract. A line that Tarley had respected, much to Ian's initial relief, then eventual disappointment. For in a bid to protect not only himself from public ridicule but Tarley from the shame of being seen holding hands with a man old enough to be his father, Ian's fear had stifled his ability to explore the beauty of what might've been.

And despite how painful it was, it was better this way.

Better, at the very least, for Tarley.

Or so it would be in the long run, once Ian had removed the temptation for both himself and his assistant. They couldn't go on like this, fancifully ignoring the elephant crowding the room. The practice would suffer, their attention to their patients depleted, with their focus shifted towards caring for an otherwise invisible animal. And besides, with the confirmation of his biopsy's initial ruling still left unknown, it was safer this way. Ian was simply being protective and proactive.

These were the lies he told himself.

The ones he repeated over and over again. While he sat in his recliner, while he lay in his bed, while he was behind the wheel of his car, and most rigorously, while he was in the vicinity of his assistant.

As he was now, standing behind Tarley, being serenaded by the internal skipping record of his rationalizations as he oversaw the administration of a routine round of vaccines. Ian's presence wasn't necessary, really. Not when Dani, the clinic's mousy vet tech, was providing more than enough assistance by holding the tiger-striped feline on the treatment table as Tarley's hands, expert and sure, inserted a needle without the patient ever offering to flinch.

"And we're done," Tarley cooed, as he pulled free the empty syringe, capped it, and handed it to Ian, then scritched the cat's forehead—all in one tender, fluid motion. It was impressive. Admirable. And warmth spread across Ian's chest as he rocked back on his heels, turning to dispose of the used needle in the sharps container.

"Is that all?" Dani asked.

"Yes, I've got it from here," Tarley assured. "Thank you."

"Sure thing." Dani gave the cat a final pat, before returning to the kennels to resume serving breakfast to the boarded dogs.

From the corner of his eye, Ian watched the kennel room's door swing shut, and though he shouldn't have, revelled in the solitude that the division of metal provided them from peering eyes and perked ears. "Have you...always held a preference for cats?" Ian asked, their backs to one another as he disposed of the vaccine vial.

"Hm?" Tarley hummed over his shoulder, stroking the cat's back until it began to radiate a bassy purr.

"You gravitate towards them. And they to you."

"It's not a preference." Tarley shrugged. "I guess I just...appreciate them."

"Why do you say that?"

"...Because I can't control them."

A startling coldness draped over Ian, a breath trapped in his chest. They hadn't spoken a word of the proposal to one another since he'd given the envelope to Tarley; and while part of Ian was willing to allow the man time to consider his offer, he felt rushed by the existential pressure of his own dread. And Ian also couldn't help from feeling like Tarley was intentionally delaying his decision—a feeling that was being exacerbated now.

"Not really, anyway," Tarley continued. "They're instinctual. More than they're emotional." Tarley steered the cat back into its carrier. "And they do what they want...even when it's not what's best for them."

Ian couldn't ignore the sharp, tingling feeling of eyes on the back of his neck. It felt like Tarley wasn't just looking at him, but seeing *through* him. He gave a measured exhale and turned around to find that Tarley was also facing him, their eyes meeting with a magnetic click. Ian held the heated gaze a beat, before venturing, "Have you put any more thought into my proposal?"

"Yes."

"And?" Ian prompted.

"I don't understand."

"The terms are clearly drawn—"

"The contract's not what I'm questioning, Doc."

Ian searched Tarley's gaze—the coaxing color of freshly steeped Earl Grey—but Tarley looked away before Ian could pick out anything distinctive from the medley of emotions swirling inside. His assistant sighed, head dropping, an action that prompted the forward motion of Tarley's feet. One step closer, then another, and the hairs on the tops of Ian's arms prickled as their eyes found one another's again, as they most always did in the seclusion of quiet rooms.

"Why me?"

Ian couldn't answer that. At least not truthfully. "You have your doctorate. You know the practice, the patients. You're...the obvious choice." Tarley's expression soured, but Ian continued anyway. "I know change is a bothersome thing, but I was really rather hoping I could retire knowing that my legacy would be left in the best of hands."

"...But why *now*?"

"Tarley, please—I'm past retirement age as it is."

"By three years. That's nothing."

"Perhaps not to you."

"Then help me understand—"

"What's not to understand?"

"Why? Why you're doing this? Retiring, I get, sure, but...dropping everything, cold turkey?" Tarley shook his head. "It's not like you. You love this place, and everyone loves you."

The word 'love' used in this context, spoken by those lips, pierced Ian to his core.

Where did Tarley's personal feelings fit into the culmination of the 'everyone' he was speaking for? And how was it those proclamations fell flat when it wasn't the majority's affection that he sought, but one man's?

Three words. That's all he wanted.

Three words that would've been strong enough to make him stay. However, Ian couldn't know if they were left unspoken because they weren't felt or because Tarley was simply adhering to boundaries that Ian, himself, had set. And besides, if Tarley did say them, it wouldn't change the indomitable fact of Ian's age, or the probability of his diagnosis—two matters that would only be hurt by such an admission, not healed.

It would be better if Tarley didn't harbor those feelings at all; the way it would be better if Ian was able to forget his own infatuations and leave them behind right along with his practice.

Frustration with the situation and himself boiled, and Ian's composure fractured as he snatched up the patient's file and slammed the folder closed. "Have you ever stopped to think that it might be easier on me this way?"

The increase in decibel, as well as the poison lacing Ian's tone, caused Tarley to stiffen.

"It's my decision to make," Ian said. "One that I already have."

"W-What? I thought you were waiting for me...Doc, you can't—"

"But I am, and I want to leave it to you—the business, the building. All of it."

The room crackled as confidence and confusion clashed, the tides turning swiftly as Tarley firmed the set of his lips into an uncomfortably tight line. The gleam in his eyes contrasted the hard set of his jaw, as did the quiver in his voice as he made a statement he very clearly didn't mean.

"...And if I don't want it?"

Ian's chest ached with the shredding of heartstrings that had no business being as sensitive as they were. He'd done this to himself. It wasn't Tarley's fault any more than it was his responsibility to salve Ian's self-inflicted wounds. Still, it burned.

"Then I suppose it wouldn't change much," Ian said, tasting the thorns of his animosity clinging to the curves of his words. He sidestepped Tarley, shoving the patient's file into his assistant's hands on his way out. "Next week will be my last, Tarley. Whether or not you've signed."

And despite the desperation of Tarley's gaze, Ian exited the treatment area, closing the door on both their conversation and any possible future they had together.

Chapter Six

The Party

Alec

HE'D NEVER CONSIDERED THE fact that Mylar balloons could be so disparaging—filling the room with more gloom than they provided brightness; a strange phenomenon with how readily they sparkled in reflective colors of silver and gold. Perhaps they were floating too close to the fluorescent lights, casting more shadows than intended. Shadows that painted the walls in the shapes of letters that spelled, in direct contrast to his feelings, the word: H-A-P-P-Y.

He'd seen Ian joyous—on days they facilitated the delivery of puppies, or when a patient with a grim prognosis showed miraculous signs of progress, or on those rare occasions when Connie brought in a batch of her grandmother's famous no-bake cookies—and despite this being one of those rare occasions, Ian Devonshire most certainly wasn't *happy*.

To the unintelligible naked eye, Ian was placid—but Alec, with his intimate knowledge of all of Ian's tells, felt the tainted air of the unsaid in every passing interaction.

The dullness of otherwise mischievous eyes.

The slightly heavier exhales of his breath.

And the distance, severely and intentionally kept.

Aside from their typical teatime, which had grown tense, the quiet painted with the absence of meaningful eye contact, Ian was withdrawn—reluctant to allow them a second of silence to spend together without the eyes of patients, owners, or co-workers lingering in the wings.

Which was exactly why, as Ian smiled and waved farewell to an Irish Setter from the exam room, Alec took the opportunity in the brief silence between one door closing and another opening, to rest his hand on Ian's forearm.

Ian's body tensed under Alec's palm, eyes deflecting. The perk of an eyebrow caused Alec to step closer into the warmth of citrus cologne, into the coldness of a barrier withstanding. Ian gently shrugged away Alec's fingers to pull off his glasses with a sigh, using the hem of his lab coat to polish already meticulously clean lenses. "What is it, Tarley?"

"Could there be a moment we have, that is just ours?" Alec whispered, his voice as fragile as a flame attempting to withstand a disparaging wind.

Ian held, seemingly struck into a stony silence by Alec's forward approach.

"We have a standing appointment," Ian reminded, before fitting back on his glasses and leaving Alec in the icy isolation of his own devices. Ian's cold shoulder was a venomous thing that made Alec feverish. The clocks on the walls seemed twice their size, ominous and mocking, counting down the menial, remaining hours they had together. Of a life, as it once existed before what would be considered everything *after*.

Didn't Ian understand that? Mourn it? Or was Alec the only one left hanging onto hope for a deflating life raft? Alec sniffled. Discontent replaced the marrow of Alec's bones as he scraped a knuckle over the moisture tracking down his cheek, brushing away the evidence.

He didn't leave the exam room, but life moved around him. Flash frames of patients, people, and every ordinary moment that made up an average workday were now amplified, saturated by the knowledge of the inevitable. These would be the minutiae he'd remember. The click of Ian's pen, the clatter of claws on the floor. Each tiny detail developing, like a photograph, into nothing but an album of memories to flip through once the instance of 'reality' had passed. But being left with only that—simply recalling Ian's fingerprints lingering on every moment of his life—wasn't enough for Alec.

He didn't want relics of this man.

He wanted the real thing.

And he looked up from his place in the back of the extravagantly decorated break room, to an impressive collection of administrative employees, vet techs, and lifelong patients (with their owners), clapping in adulation as Ian bowed appreciatively to the crowd. Confetti floated down in slow motion, hands coming together and apart with the rhythm of languid waves, while the knife in Ian's scabbed-over hand sliced expertly, though painfully, through the word 'congratulations' sprawled in bright red frosting across the top of a rectangular cake.

Distantly, Alec realized he wasn't clapping, but he couldn't bring himself to—especially not when Ian looked up at him from across the room and boldly met his gaze. Something in Alec shattered. Not because of his own fragility, but of what he saw reflected in Ian—a countdown to an emotional implosion, as the Doctor's complexion paled and his eyes misted.

His duty to react was inescapable and Alec was moving before he realized, weaving between the bodies of the crowd to the honorary table at the front of the room. He was at Ian's side within an instant, his heart stuttering with the nearness that hadn't been allowed for almost a week. But Alec was appreciative of the weight leaning back onto his palm as he pressed it discreetly to the dip in Ian's lower back, steadying the pillar that, to him, was so clearly crumbling. He slipped the knife from Ian's grasp.

Alec then tipped his head to Connie, who had also taken a concerned initiative step forward. "Would you mind serving everyone?" Alec smiled and asked, offering her the crumb-coated utensil.

"Sure thing, Boss."

"Yes...save us a corner piece, will you?" Ian said, distantly, before turning away at Alec's careful guidance.

Alec, without allowing himself the time to digest Ian's public use of the word *us*, ushered them from the room and into the adjacent privacy of the boarding kennels. He gave Ian's lower back a little push, soft as sending off a paper boat, before turning to secure the door behind them. His hand stayed on the knob, unwilling to turn around as he listened to the shuddered quality of Ian's breathing. Alec closed his eyes, and let his forehead linger near the stability of the closed door, willing the quality of the metal to fuse with his molecules and give him the strength to withstand this moment.

"I...I just needed a minute," Ian admitted, after a prolonged silence.

"I know."

In their kennels, the dogs stood up from their beds, tails wagging in anticipation of affection from the physicians. The sound of their nails scraping on the metal filled the quiet, and Alec let his grip loosen on the knob.

"I don't know what came over me," Ian sighed.

Alec's brow bunched as he recalled the sureness with which Ian had accepted the congratulations of his retirement until he was met with the insistence of the singular gaze he'd been avoiding since the start; the evidence of who he was hurting by making this decision. Apparently, the truth of the carnage that cutting himself from a person who needed him had become too real, too overwhelming. That, or Ian had suddenly been faced with his own denial of all the reasons he had to stay.

"I do," Alec whispered.

"...How?"

His mouth spread into a hesitant, sad smile, and he turned away from the door, reluctant to meet the gaze he felt boring at him from across the expanse of the too-small room. Alec took to rubbing his hands together and caught himself examining the emptiness between the knuckles of the ring finger on his left hand.

He took one conscientious step towards Ian, then one more.

"Doc...did you ever wonder why I never married?"

"W-What?" Ian stuttered, abhorred. "No. Absolutely not."

"Why?"

"...Such private concerns are not mine to meddle in."

"They are when you're part of their reason."

Alec dared to look up, catching Ian's graying expression. The man seemed to struggle with this knowledge, like trying to hold a hot potato without scalding oneself by letting the weight of it linger and, God forbid, sink in.

Ian cleared his throat and firmed his gaze. "That's preposterous."

"Is it?"

"It...It's too late, Tarley."

"How? How is it too late?"

A spark of recognition lit Ian's eyes and a crease cut between his brows. "You...haven't signed the proposal?"

"Neither have you," Alec pointed out, unhelpfully.

And Ian shook his head as Alec drifted closer, then closer still.

"But...I've made my announcement," Ian said.

"So have I."

The prominent apple of Ian's throat bobbed, but he held his ground as Alec stopped with only an arm's width between them. The air swirled and behind them the dogs paced, whimpering, charged by the uncertain energy being bolstered by the men in the room.

"Haven't I?" Alec asked, seeking clarification of what he'd so vaguely revealed, hoping it would be enough.

And although Ian seemed to understand the underhanded nature of Alec's inference, the Doctor distanced, tucking his chin to his chest, whispering, "There are rules we must follow to be proper people."

Alec's heart stalled at the sear of such a weak rejection.

"I don't want to be proper," he countered, his tone souring like the lining of his stomach. "I don't want to be safe. Or simple. Or sane."

His fingers reached out, taking desperate hold of Ian's arms as Alec stumbled out onto a ledge that only a heartsick few ever returned from.

"I want to be in love. Which I am. With you."

Ian's gaze leveled him—shock, desire, and fright melding together in a furious fire that left Alec completely burned as the Doctor pursed his lips into a tight line of repentance.

"You can't say things like that."

"Like what—the truth? Would you rather I lie?"

"Maybe I would."

"Because you'd rather not know or because you'd rather not admit that you feel it, too?"

A piercing bark caused Ian to jump and instead of forcing their contact, Alec dropped his trembling fingers from Ian's arms.

He stepped back.

Ian remained, not chasing him—and Alec scolded himself for hoping he would.

"What does it gain you, telling me this? Now, of all times?"

Alec's chin crinkled and he raked his fingers through the salted chocolate of his hair, breaking the composure he'd so carefully kept—finally allowing his exterior to mirror the disheveled nature of his soul. "Doc, I could make a shorter list of everything I'd be losing if I just kept my mouth shut."

Ian's jaw tightened and his eyes fell to the floor. "I know you're not a foolish man. But you're very mistaken if you think you could ever gain anything from me beyond my burden—"

"It's not a burden if I want to carry it!" Alec snapped, and the dogs rattled the bars of their cages; the pressure mounting as shrill yips and throaty barks echoed in a treacherous tornado around them, but Alec could only focus on driving his point home.

"You don't get it, do you?" Alec exhaled shakily, his voice barely audible above the cacophony of the dogs bawling for attention in the same way he had, for all these years, yearned for Ian's.

And now that he was daring to make this jump, Alec decided that if he was going to fall—if Ian wasn't going to catch him—then he didn't want the salvation of a parachute. "You're not a burden. You're far from it. You're refined, you—"

"Stop!"

"—have your life together, you—"

"Tarley, please—"

"—know what you want—"

"What I *want* is for you to leave me alone!" Ian bit back, shoving past Alec, who was reaching for him.

"Why? So you can be alone with your unhappiness?"

"No!" Ian bellowed above the canine clamor. "So I can have a moment of silence in which to hear myself think!"

He hadn't expected Ian to answer, much less do so honestly. And only because Ian had said it was what he wanted, Alec had full intention of letting him go.

It hurt to allow Ian to storm from the room and slam the door, but Alec was thankful that he wasn't left alone with the deafening sound of his own heart breaking. Instead, he was cocooned in the croons of concerned animals, who were no more certain of what had just happened than he was.

Alec turned towards the cages, raising a placating palm.

"Shhh," he breathed, attempting to calm their anxieties while trying to tame his own. But those fears were fierce and feral, and Alec knelt onto the ground, cupping his hands over his face to shelter himself from the shame of trying to cage a wild thing, and failing. His shushing morphed into the shudders of sobs as Alec keened, dragging his hands down the front of the cages while the animals inside whimpered alongside him, and licked the salt from his fingers.

Chapter Seven

The Announcement

Ian

SECOND ONLY TO THE sound of his own heart beating, the shudder of that slamming door was the most profound resonation that Ian had ever heard; and he regretted it immediately. There had been a permanence to it that Ian prayed that Tarley wouldn't honor, because although he hadn't meant it to be a decisive measure, he didn't have the fortitude to turn around and make it right.

Running was cowardly, he knew, but it was necessary for self-preservation, as years' worth of self-built lies were washed out by the blinding light of Tarley's truth—one that Ian had been in denial of, just as much as he was paralyzed by the fear of its sudden existence.

Finding shelter in the seclusion of his office, Ian slunk down into one of those wingback chairs, pried off his glasses, and washed a hand over his face, pondering about how childish it was of him to flee. Every interaction that they'd had over the last eight years played in flash frames across his mind, and Ian groaned at the obviousness of it all, tortured by the ignorance of his former, fearful self in light of the man that he was now—still terrified, but at least enlightened.

However, in this specific instance, knowledge did not feel like power, but like a straitjacket that bound him up in previously drawn lines and with the expectations of a world that wouldn't understand them. Much less accept them. How could he expect acceptance, when even he, himself, was struggling with the morality of his desires? He'd wanted Tarley's love for so very long, and now that it was being actualized, he didn't know how to accept it.

How Tarley could be so contrite was far beyond Ian—for shame was a thicket of brambles that once breached, left remnants clinging to skin and clothes. He couldn't escape what history had impressed upon him or what small-mountain-town-society deemed as appropriate conduct for an elderly businessman and his middle-aged employee. And at the very heart of it, Ian couldn't bear the thought of telling Tarley he loved him from one side of his mouth, then immediately admitting that he had cancer from the other.

There was comfort to be found in a routine, which was why, even with his hands shaking, Ian allowed autopilot to guide him to the kettle. He shouldn't have been expecting those three quiet knocks on his office door, the way he shouldn't have been expecting Tarley to want the same things that he did. Yet he found himself glancing up at the clock as he laid their usual array of biscuits out on their usual serving plate in the hopes that monotony would mend the irreparable damage he'd caused.

It was safe to assume that the party was still commencing in the break room despite lacking its guest of honor. Ian was wrought with guilt for his disappearing act and vehemently hoped that all these transgressions wouldn't spoil the day. Hopes that were bolstered when, past the gurgle of the kettle, Ian discerned the faint approach of familiar feet. His heart leapt with the coveted cadence of those three knocks.

Ian's eyes flicked to the clock hanging on the wall. It was four p.m. on the dot.

"Come in."

The door creaked open, and silently, Tarley slipped inside.

Without diverting his attention to the door, Ian went about tending to the teapot, letting his auditory senses track Tarley's slower-than-usual movements as he timidly stepped into the office but did not move to help Ian, nor to take a seat. By the sound of it, he was keeping his distance, acting like the unwanted stranger that Ian had, no doubt, made him feel. Ian closed his eyes for a moment, hunched over the serving tray, gathering himself and mustering all of the courage he'd failed to present earlier. Exhaling a controlled breath, Ian left the tea set where it was and turned to face Tarley, who was standing on the opposite side of the sitting area, wringing his hands.

"I'm terribly sorry," Ian offered.

"I'm sorry, too."

"Whatever for?"

"For waiting."

Ian paused for a beat, then nodded, watching as Tarley neared, his movements strikingly similar to that of a beaten dog, and Ian hated that he was the master of the usually confident man's newfound trepidation.

"It could've been easier, if—"

"It wouldn't have been any easier, Tarley. Don't fool yourself into falling for regret."

Their gazes met, and Ian was faced with the evidence of what he'd left behind when he'd slammed that door. The puffy redness of those wondrous eyes spoke volumes to the hurt he'd laid, and Ian thought that the sight alone was more painful than anything Tarley could've said, but he was wrong.

"That's exactly what I was trying to avoid," Tarley whispered.

And Ian's stomach dropped with the weight of being force-fed the guilt of both rejecting Tarley when he hadn't wanted to and how inelegantly he'd chosen to do it.

Ian could feel the blood draining from his features, but he couldn't bring himself to speak—what was he to say to justify the means of his cruelty? His silence, he thought, was more appropriate. Giving Tarley a chance to speak what Ian had otherwise muzzled was more important now than bandaging his own hemorrhaging wounds. So, Ian stood, still and quiet.

This gave Tarley the conviction to move forward, which he did, but not to meet Ian at the worktop. He slid down into his usual wingback chair with a shaking exhale, pinning his elbows to his knees and dragging his fingers through stress-havocked hair. "Just when I had worked up the courage, now you...you spite me, and plan to take it all away."

"Quite the contrary," Ian interjected, immediately forgetting his vow of silence. "I plan to leave you my legacy."

"You are the legacy I want, not this office."

Ian shook his head, staring down at the wrinkled, bruised, and scabbed-over hands that were somehow his, clasped politely at his navel. "I'm ancient history—"

Tarley scoffed, his appetite for pleasantries apparently worn thin. "Aren't we all in the end?"

Grim as it might've seemed, Ian agreed. That was, after all, one of the main sources of his contention against this union. But Ian simply hung his head, unwilling to enact a firefight with stubborn logic.

Their eyes refused to meet, and the room simmered, not so unlike the leaves left steeping in the pot.

The clock on the wall ticking was omnipresent, and Ian was all too aware of the uneven quality of his breathing. He wanted Tarley to say something. Anything, at this point. But the man was certainly full of surprises, for Ian didn't expect him to stand.

Tarley shifted from the seat, drawing Ian's gaze. From the interior pocket of his lab coat, Tarley withdrew a notorious-looking envelope that had seen some better days. The top was ripped haphazardly open, the edges worn and crinkled from being stuffed too long in pockets too near to troubled hearts. He advanced with a firmness that Ian remembered, but one that was curious now, as he stuck out the letter for Ian to take.

"I signed it," Tarley said.

Yet, Ian did not immediately accept the letter. Instead, he spent a long beat staring into those bloodshot eyes, facing the man who had, until this moment, kept considerable distance between them. This felt like a truce; though a false one.

Ian hesitantly accepted the letter and ran his thumb across it, consideringly. "I thought you didn't want this."

Tarley frowned, gesturing with his now-free hand as he stepped back towards the sitting area. "I don't want you to leave. There's a difference." He puddled down into the chair. "But the least I can do is give you what you want, even if I can't have what I want, too."

It was one thing to understand when someone was wrong and another thing entirely to convince them of a perceived truth. As much as Alec Tarley wanted to believe, for some mistaken reason that Ian was a flawless man, Tarley was only setting himself up for disappointment. Because now, on top of all the mounting pressures that came from the threats to his health and the longevity of his career, Ian was being forced to confess aloud what he otherwise would have kept buried. This was his penance, he supposed. If accepting the proposal was the least that Tarley could do, then being honest was the least Ian could afford.

"You're grossly mistaken about one thing, Tarley. About me."

"What's that, Doc?"

"I don't know what I want. Not for certain. Only that...what I want I cannot have."

Tarley shook his head. "I think you're denying yourself your own happiness."

"No. I'm saving you."

"From what?"

"From me."

"Doc, I—"

"I have cancer, Tarley."

He hadn't meant to say it, to blurt out what wasn't yet confirmed, but the worst-case scenario that had been plaguing like storm clouds in the back of his mind, since the day they'd taken the biopsy, tumbled out before he could stop the landslide. Tarley looked stricken, utterly crushed, and Ian was crippled with the consternation of having confessed his greatest fear for the first time out loud.

"W-What?" Tarley pushed up from the chair and staggered forward, his former coldness forgotten as he took a more customary position in Ian's immediacy. His hand found Ian's arm, and Ian shook his head.

"Or...or it's possible I do. They're waiting on a second opinion. And, beyond that, I have maybe twenty years left. Maybe? If I'm lucky." Ian's trembling hand rested over Tarley's, the other holding the shivering letter. "You've got so many more ahead of you. So much more potential to reach. I'd be nothing better to you than a...a...an anchor."

Tarley's eyes softened, his lips quivering into a smile. "But that's exactly what I'm looking for."

Ian's throat cinched, heated with the remorse of all these cumulative blunders. He couldn't bear to do this again, to say those words again if and when the news finally came. His voice cracked, and Ian eased towards Tarley's comfort, not away. "Please—"

"The future doesn't mean anything to me if you're not in it," Tarley begged.

"That's what I'm trying to tell you, Tarley. I'll die before you."

"Doc," Tarley grounded, shaking his head. He then gently took the letter from Ian's hand and tucked it under the serving tray behind them on the worktop. Their attentions returned to one another, laser focused. Tarley reached to cup his palm over Ian's cheek. It was the closest they had ever been, and the warmth in Tarley's eyes advertised just how much he was savoring the moment.

"That's not guaranteed," Tarley said. "Nothing is. Except right here. Right now."

Ian knew that Tarley was right. He'd spent so long worrying about crossing the bridges yet to come that he'd let the one he was standing on rot and collapse out from under him. Everything that he had been trying to preemptively fix, ensure, or resist had come to fruition anyway. Despite his best efforts not to, he'd become one of the unlucky few to develop cancer. And despite his best efforts not to, he'd fallen in love with his assistant.

He couldn't mend the past, couldn't apply more sunscreen or accept Tarley's long-since expired invitation to afternoon tea outside office hours. But what Ian could do was take advantage of the now—without allowing his fear to turn would've, could'ves, and should'ves into instantaneous regrets.

The brush of Tarley's fingers was a soothing balm on skin long dehydrated of such compassions, and his learned inclination to flinch away from it, combated with his instinct to lean into it. For the first time in more than half his life, Ian allowed himself to give in to what it was he wanted, not what he thought he should have, or what someone else deserved. He rested his cheek into Tarley's hand, and Tarley's eyes sparkled with a delight that, for the last two weeks, Ian had so severely missed.

"How do we know if it's too late?" Ian asked.

"I guess we won't." He gave a little shrug. "Not for certain. But...we won't know if we never try." Tarley's head tilted, his gaze as tender as his touch. "Do you want to do that? To try with me?" He sounded so sincere, and Ian went lightheaded when Tarley's other hand rested against his hip. "I want that."

Those honeyed eyes flickered from where their gazes met, down to his lips. Ian simultaneously flushed and felt faint. He didn't know what to say, how to conduct himself, where to put his hands. This wasn't like him—like *them*—and his lack of experience in this area caused him to falter, forgetting to breathe. Ian inhaled sharply and Tarley took it as a cue; he recoiled slightly, self-conscious, asking, "What is it about me that you don't want?"

Ian peered into those reddened eyes, and it was then he realized that he hadn't just been committing a crime against himself, but involuntarily against the man he held great feelings for. The entire time that he'd been denying himself the pleasure of being with this man, he'd been blind to the unspeakable pressures and expectations he'd put on Tarley to be someone he was not.

All this time, as tactfully as he'd been able to, Tarley had attempted to become known, and Ian, scared by what-ifs, clipped the wings of a falcon before it ever learned to fly. And now that it was fully grown, a sentient thing with desires and dreams of its own, what sort of monster would Ian be to look a wild thing in the eyes—to see himself reflected in them—and ask it to remain grounded.

It deserved freedom.

And so did they.

"Nothing," Ian admitted. "I very much want every part of you."

"Then have me."

Ian recognized a look in Tarley's eyes that, like a crimson rose with all its thorns, was beautiful in its danger. Alluring, inviting, romantic, and homey in ways he couldn't understand. These were the emotions swirling in the colors of those tea-steeped eyes, and Ian's breath caught as he realized his vision was blurring. *No.* His glasses were fogging.

Tarley had leaned forward an incremental amount to allow the tips of their noses to touch, but the rest of the distance was Ian's to close. And despite the fear that threatened to stall him from bridging the gap, Ian rocked forward until their lips met.

Ian embraced the feeling; slowly at first, then wholeheartedly.

Tarley's left hand firmed against his waist once more, while the fingers of his right combed through the hair over Ian's ear, mussing the careful style the Doctor normally kept. Ian didn't notice—couldn't care—inhibited by the taste of Tarley, the likes of which he'd only ever dreamed.

Yet, his dreams had never been as good as this.

Their chests were heaving, hearts bounding, when they finally parted, and Tarley's lips split into a wolfish grin. Absently, Ian wondered what new flavors such a smile might have injected into those lips; and while he'd never been one for such affections before, he found himself bearing a keen desire to explore them now.

Ian's tongue flickered out over his lips, and he was suddenly aware of how warm his face felt. Tarley tentatively leaned forward, but Ian startled back, shy.

"We'll spoil our appetite for cake."

Tarley combed a strand of Ian's hair back into place.

"That's alright, isn't it? That's not what we're celebrating anymore."

Chapter Eight

Aftermath

Alec

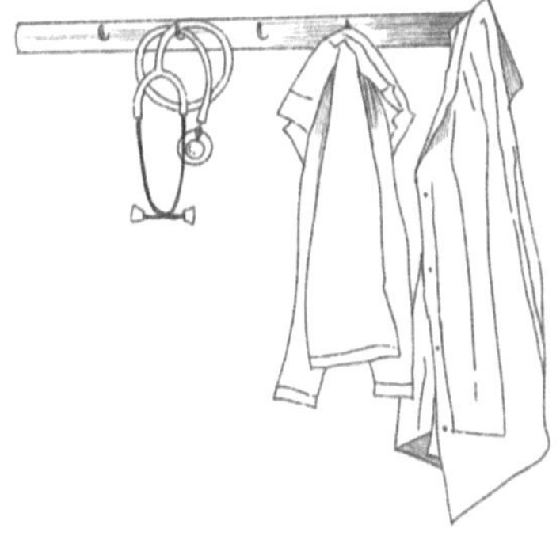

IT WAS, FOR ALL intents and purposes, a typical Monday; but the sky had never been so blue. The crisp morning air curled in through the Jeep's open windows as Alec wound down the highway. The mountainous road was aflame on either side with the eruption of the equinox falling into full, unapologetic bloom.

He'd driven this route countless times, and although he anticipated the well-known vistas hiding behind every corner, Alec marveled at the world around him like he was experiencing it for the first time. And in many ways, he was.

Because the moment his lips met Ian's, the timeline of his existence had branched into a stark division of everything that happened before, and everything that came after. That kiss, and every soft connection that had then so slowly followed, became the lenses through which Alec now viewed the world; and it, while already being quite a lovely life, surmounted itself.

Of course, he'd dared to dream what a life on the other side of an after might look like—but it had always been a distant sort of visualization with the opacity of smoke, elusively lingering just outside of his hopeful reach. Alec had found his courage while stumbling in the dark of that desolate place between losing Ian for now and losing Ian for good, and against all odds, he'd captured it. But now that he had, Alec realized he never would've maintained a vivid enough imagination to accurately predict just how differently it would feel to be standing on the other side of it—how good it would feel to have those affections not only known, but reciprocated. Where every beat of his heart was firmer, every laugh heartier, and every single moment was doused in the intensity of a tangerine haze.

Alec couldn't stop replaying the moment that they'd shared in Ian's office, and couldn't stifle the spread of a smile that accompanied the memory each time, either. A vibrancy had been pumped into him and with so much novelty to explore, Alec didn't want to lose sight of the fork in the road that had brought him here—a reminiscence that he had visited more in the last forty-eight hours than he maybe should have.

But it was hard not to allow himself to linger there, in the memory of that glorious moment with Ian, when it had been the ecstasy of a waking dream that not even pinching himself could disturb him from. The delicate skin of his inner forearm was dappled with the little, brown bruises of such efforts, and while Alec knew that this was real, he *still* found it difficult to convince his brain of what had, for so long, been categorized as nothing more than an impossibility.

And now, he'd been inside Ian's home.

It was just as charming as he'd always imagined it—all rich woods and cozy furnishings in a quaint, classic A-frame, set back from the road. It had a detached garage and a row of raised gardens out back. Much like Ian's office, it was orderly and inviting, and, beyond that, Alec couldn't remember much else about the house when he'd been too engrossed in memorizing details about the man sitting across from him instead.

Who was Ian Devonshire outside the walls of their clinic?

They hadn't spent much of their dinner that evening discussing the terms of the contract or the medical complications that Ian had briefly admitted—and not on the basis that Alec didn't want to discuss them. In fact, Alec wanted very badly to ask Ian what he'd meant about the cancer, to learn how he knew and how long he'd lived alone with such a secret, but whatever they had was fragile. He didn't want to risk breaking it while the attainment of his gamble remained a precarious miracle that he wanted to treasure, not drive off.

So, they didn't discuss the uncertainty of their future, nor the time that had been wasted by the uncoordinated dancing they'd done around the truth in their past. Instead, they focused on the tingling sensation evidently felt by both men as they sat across from each other at the kitchen table, sharing a pot of afterdinner tea, while Alec appreciated those olive eyes and teased his socked foot down the Doctor's shin.

Ian hadn't pulled away.

Alec was so high on the adrenaline of sinking heart-first into the promise of whatever this could grow into that he hadn't anticipated the savage gutting he'd experience when pulling into the clinic's parking lot. The saturation of his world drained away into melancholy monochromes. For, while he always made the stringent point to arrive early as a means to prepare the rooms for Ian and their first round of patients, Alec realized, as he killed the engine of his Jeep, that his punctuality wouldn't matter—because Ian wasn't coming.

The walk through the leaf-littered parking lot was garrulous and slow, though not nearly as agonizing to cross as the threshold of the clinic's back door. The hallway seemed to stretch for long, lonely miles, and Alec was drained by the time he turned into the break room at the far end, where he hung up his bag in a cubby and began to shoulder off his denim jacket to replace it with his lab coat.

"Aren't you going to put that in your office?"

Connie's voice startled him from his dispirited stupor, and Alec jumped, turning to look over his shoulder. He perked an eyebrow at her suggestion. He didn't have a personal off—

"*Oh.* Right." Alec's jaw was tight from her gentle coaxing.

Although he knew she was only trying to encourage him to take advantage of what he'd apparently earned, it felt as though she were, unintentionally or not, prodding the rawness of an open wound.

He slung both of his coats over his arm and gathered his bag before turning to where she was leaning with one shoulder against the door jamb, her warm eyes assessing him. He squeezed past her and returned to the hallway, which had somehow elongated further. His destination seemed unreachable, the finish line furthering with each step until suddenly he was upon it, standing, staring at the swirling grains of the heavy wood.

And for the first time, Alec entered this office without knocking, only because he knew that there would be no one there to permit him from the other side.

The door creaked open, and a knot firmed in his gut when he found the office shrouded in a dull, unusual shadow. The blinds of the far windows were shut. He'd only ever entered this space after they had been twirled open by what Tarley had never realized, until now, were caring and diligent hands. He'd taken Ian's attention to detail for granted and Tarley was now stalled, hand curled over the brass doorknob as he examined the office for the traces of Ian that remained as a result of his voluntary but rapid eviction.

Exhaling a shivering breath, Tarley stepped inside and crossed the familiar space, seeing it through new eyes. Taking in everywhere that Ian should have been but wasn't, and everywhere he lingered, despite.

He sat his messenger bag and collection of coats down in a pile on the desk and tended to the windows, letting the gilded, autumn sun cast the room in shades of gold. Tarley's eye was caught by an errant glimmer of something across the room, where atop that low filing cabinet, the holly-painted tea set still reverently sat on its silver platter. It seemed to wink knowingly at him as it gleamed in the dawning light; and Tarley's throat constricted, tears stinging at the corners of his eyes as he recalled, for the millionth time in nearly seventy-two hours, that this was the exact spot where, without ever expressly saying the words, Ian had confessed his love.

A knock on the door caused Tarley to swallow the thick lump of fuzzy, tepid emotion tangled in his throat, and he dragged a finger under his eye to ensure the moisture was gone prior to turning and answering, "Come in."

He hadn't shut the door completely, and Dani squeaked the passage open only a fraction more, enough to duck their head in. "Doctor," they said, perhaps out of a newfound respect for his position or out of an unfortunate habit. Tarley schooled a wince. "Your first patient is in exam one."

"Great." He smiled, and cleared his throat to rid the rasp from his voice. "I'll be right there."

Which he was, swiftly, only after tugging on his lab coat and saddling a stethoscope around his neck—all too grateful for the distraction of a busy schedule. And while it was easier than he anticipated to fall into a rhythm with the tech, there was always something amiss in the balance of the universe they were recreating; like a cold spot that lingered, an emptiness that prevailed despite Ian's attempt to supplement Tarley in his place.

More than once, a patient's owner called him 'Dr. Devonshire'.

More than once, he glanced to gift a smile at Ian, forgetting he wasn't there to receive it.

And by the afternoon, Tarley was exhausted, his emotional weakness bleeding into a physical one. He collapsed into a chair in the break room, rubbing his weary eyes until white splotches floated around like snowflakes. Through the static flurries, he glanced about the break room, which had been dismantled of its jolly decorations. All that remained was a white cake box with sparse scraps and beside: a paper plate with Saran wrap stretched over the top of a sizable corner piece.

The slice they'd never partaken in and had subsequently forgotten.

The edges of Tarley's lips quivered up into a garish smile as he chuckled, not only at the thought of what they'd otherwise indulged in, but at the testament of Connie's commendation.

Tarley sighed, combing back some loose curls from his forehead as he stood and glanced at the clock on the wall. There was still time.

"Hey, Connie," Tarley said, as he stuck his head in from around the corner of the hallway to where she was sitting at the front desk.

She spun around in her chair and clever eyes flickered between the denim jacket Tarley had on and the packed-up plate of cake he had balanced in one hand.

She smirked at him. "Yeah, Boss?"

"I'm stepping out for a little bit."

"What for?" she teased.

And his cheeks glowed, but not with embarrassment. He colored with the satisfaction of her knowing and his ability to say, without abandon, and with a bolstered conviction: "A standing appointment."

Chapter Nine

Four O'Clock

Ian

IF IAN WAS HONEST with himself, there had always been rumblings—faint as they might've been.

At first, he had simply thought that Tarley's warmth was wholesale, his affectionate nature a free-range thing that would nudge its head into the hand of anyone bold enough to approach the fence. However, as months culminated into years, and an over-qualified assistant became his practical shadow, Ian allowed himself to become percipient to the then-obvious truth surrounding the source of the sparks produced by even the subtlest of touches.

They weren't coming from the limitations caging Tarley in.

They were coming from Tarley.

And now that he had been released from the constrictive confines of Ian's imposed boundaries, Tarley's robust and wonderful disposition revealed itself with a startling vivacity. Ian was taken aback, swept off his feet by the tenderness exposed where a hard callous had previously been protecting the sensitivity of a feral heart that wanted nothing more than to be domesticated.

Tarley's love was a dissonance—though not an entirely unpleasant one.

It was just that it had been so very long since anyone besides Ian had been past the threshold of this house, much less welcomed into it to make use of the furniture. Though, as strange as it was to have another living being within the wood-paneled walls of his home, Ian found that the moment the front door closed, and he was left alone without Tarley's tenacious energy invigorating the space, the silence swelled. The emptiness became oppressive; and Ian realized, as he sank into his chair beside the crackling fire, that it always had been.

Much like he'd fooled himself into believing that Tarley didn't want him, or worse yet, that he would be perceived as a blemish on Tarley's reputation, Ian had spent decades lying to himself that his home was his sanctuary. In reality, it wasn't his home that he was running to, but the emptiness of it that he was escaping from. The clinic—and moreover, the man with whom he shared his days within it—was where Ian had truly planted the seeds of his peace and now, despite fearing the failure of the crop they had nurtured, Tarley was going to be there with him when it was time to sow.

A harvest he continued to grapple with the terror of reaping, no matter how assuring Tarley tried to, and often succeeded, at being in convincing Ian that he was worthy of this. Deserving of it, too. Because Ian felt aloof, irrevocably hardwired to see rain clouds where Tarley only ever spotted rainbows; and for that, Ian was simultaneously thankful and ashamed. He didn't want to be that way, but it was a carefully curated defense mechanism that he didn't know how to disable now that he didn't need it anymore.

Or, at least, not while Tarley was around.

Which he wasn't. Ian had made the irrevocable mistake of supplementing a terrible distance between them by making the rash decision to retire without fully taking into account the scope of the ramifications he'd be subjecting himself to. Like the damnation of solitude to the claustrophobic quiet of this empty house.

Morning was the hardest as it crept, sad and slow, over the horizon to peek into his window. Ian hadn't slept, and he watched sunlight slink across the backyard, a reminder of all the places he didn't have to go. And while part of him thought he might as well get dressed and comb his hair, then drive to the clinic and continue his life like no such decree had ever been made, the more rational side of his brain knew that such reckless thinking was what had gotten him into this derelict situation in the first place.

He compromised by getting out of bed, but by not driving to the clinic, as he'd done every weekday—holidays withstanding—for more than three-quarters of his life.

Time trudged slowly while his mind raced; regret a noose he hadn't realized he was about to hang himself with. He was jittery, idle hands shook with the rush of too much caffeine as he mindlessly made and sipped, and made and sipped, pot after pot of black tea with absolutely nowhere to put the energy beyond faster-paced worrying while he ponged between boredom and waiting for the phone to ring.

It never did.

However, Ian was torn from the pages of his long-neglected mass-market paperback when he discerned the distinct but odd insistence of three raps at his front door, cutting through the laze of the late afternoon. With a heavily knitted brow, Ian sat his book aside, pushed up from his chair, and shuffled across the room.

He'd never been happier to answer a door.

"Tarley?" Ian exhaled the name on a breath that was punched from his gut with equal blows of shock and surprise. "What're you doing here?"

Tarley simply tilted his head, adjusted the bundle in his hand, and offered a benevolent smile. "Well, it's four o'clock, isn't it?"

Ian blinked, twisting around to look from where he was standing in the doorway to the grandfather clock across the room and not moments later, it began to chime. "Why, y-yes, but—"

"We haven't missed teatime together in ten years. I don't intend to start now."

"Eight years—"

"And four months. I know," Tarley corrected Ian's correction, his eyes glittering. "But I find it easier if we just round up." A rush of heat clapped the back of Ian's neck, and he smiled, smoothing a hand down the front of his jumper, thankful he'd had the wherewithal to get himself dressed.

Tarley rocked his weight foot to foot and peered around Ian. "Can I come in?"

"Ah!" Ian shook his head to dislodge the thick cobwebs that had grown across his common sense as he'd been stuck staring at Tarley—afraid that if he blinked, the mirage would vanish. "Yes. Please." He stepped aside and tossed out an arm, indicatively. "Please do."

"Thank you." Tarley bowed his head and stepped inside, pausing by the front door to toe off his shoes. Ian hadn't instructed this measure but admired the care with which Tarley tucked his sneakers aside and then sought permission before entering further into the house. Ian nodded and followed Tarley to where he was meandering to the kitchen—as if he'd forgotten where it was or didn't want to make it so obvious that he already knew the way.

"What's that you've brought?" Ian asked.

"Cake. Connie packed it for us."

Ian stopped stone-cold in the middle of the green carpet, watching as Tarley rounded the butcher block island and sat the offering down. Tarley's movements were loose and unbothered by this revelation and the insinuation with which Connie had packaged the treat.

"Us?" Ian ventured.

And Tarley's gaze rose to meet Ian's, as he pulled back the wrapping to reveal a section cut big enough for two to comfortably share. "Yes."

Ian observed the ease with which Tarley dismantled the barriers that had been built out of a necessity to hide, while Ian remained cowering behind the sturdy structure of his own. It was foolish and unnecessary to be concerned about being caught while in the privacy of his own home, and belittling to believe that he'd concern himself with the opinions of others, anyway. Yet, it was a difficult tendency to just...let go.

Tarley's bravery was exemplary, but it wasn't pressurized—he didn't chastise or encourage Ian. He simply approached the situation with a silent steadiness that Ian found comforting. And hopeful.

It was the warm solidity of Tarley's gaze that melted Ian from where he'd been frozen by the fear that their infatuation would falter when tried by a stranger's scrutiny. Though Ian was now confident that whatever surety he needed, Tarley intended to carry for him in a well-stocked supply.

"You've impeccable timing," Ian said, as he joined Tarley in the kitchen. "I've just put the kettle on."

Tarley chuckled. "I could really use the pick-me-up, Doc," Tarley said as Ian passed him a knife to divvy up the cake before pulling down a set of small serving plates from the cupboard.

"Typical Monday?" Ian asked.

Tarley shook his head, his eyes going soft-edged as they turned to meet Ian's. "Not exactly."

I missed you, too.

He couldn't bring himself to say the words, even though they clung to the tip of his tongue.

Something about the way that energy charged between the lock of their gazes made Ian aware that Tarley understood—if only because Tarley was saying it, without saying it, too.

The warmth of a hand on his lower back caused a momentary tension to prickle along his spine, but Ian relaxed quickly into the touch. They stood there in a silence that no longer threatened to strangle but instead propagated an air of intimacy that Ian had only ever known in the isolation of exam rooms. It was a marvelous feeling to let Tarley's adjacency linger while they occupied a room with windows—even though there were little more than the birds and the pines to see them. Still, Ian allowed that tiny pebble of pride to feel like a mountain moved, because to him, it was.

Tarley smiled down at him and reclaimed his hand, utilizing it to plate the now-cut pieces of cake. Ian tended to the teapot, and the kitchen took on an ebb and flow not so dissimilar to the one that carried them in the office. Once the plates were set with dessert forks, Tarley turned to carry them to the kitchen table. When Ian noticed, a little noise of protest shot from his lips, loud enough to cause Tarley to pause mid-step and glance over his shoulder, as if he'd gone out of bounds and done something wrong.

Ian swallowed nervously, glancing from Tarley to where the sliding glass door, leading to the garden, was letting ample sunlight in. "It's so lovely outside..." he started, the creased edges of his mouth twitching into a grin. "I thought, maybe, we could sit on the patio?"

The weight of the suggestion hung in the air, and Tarley, usually so sure-footed, appeared to have been caught off guard, paling as he turned to better face Ian and the decision left in his court.

"Oh." Tarley glanced down at the plates, then to the exposure of the space where Ian had proposed they take their tea, while the flutter of his lashes complimented his bashful smile. "Sure."

Delight spiraled through Ian at the awareness of an acceptance—a feeling that he gathered Tarley shared, but for different reasons. This would be the first time, aside from the clinic's parking lot, that they'd be together in a public space. Even if that 'public space' was simply Ian's non-fenced-in back garden. Ian unlocked and slid open the door for Tarley before following shortly after with the tea tray.

The decking was sturdy but aged, with a few steps leading out to a vast garden, ringed by a forest of maple and pine. Although the sun continued to shine, the patio was shaded, and the air was sharp with the flavors of autumn—their teacups steaming readily as Ian fixed them up. A little wooden side table was tucked between a set of rocking chairs, one that was well worn and the other, dusty. Tarley took an unprecedented seat despite Ian's initial look of concern and seemed comfortable as he tested the unused rocker's dexterity and admired the forest encircling the house.

Ian was dissolving a lump of sugar in each cup when he noticed from the corner of his eye that Tarley had stopped rocking in his chair...and was looking at him. "What is it?"

"Have they called yet?"

Ian stopped stirring, allowing for the quiet rustle of wind in the pines to be the answer that Tarley craved. But sometimes, no news was good news. And sometimes, no news was the worst news of all.

"No." Ian swallowed and began stirring again.

He hadn't allowed himself to think beyond this moment, then the very next. Too afraid to cast his sights too far forward, to a place where Tarley wouldn't be. Which was ironic, considering that Tarley ought to have been the one afraid of being left behind. Ian turned to hand Tarley his teacup, and their fingers grazed as Tarley accepted it—however, the touch lingered, because Ian didn't let go. Their eyes met.

"They will," Tarley promised.

"I know."

Until that phone call, Ian was as healthy as Schrödinger's Cat. And that was a plausible deniability he wanted to prolong as much as possible, no matter how imminent it and the probable outcome was.

Confident that Tarley had the teacup, Ian let go and sank down into his own rocker, though left his tea steaming on the table. For a considerable time, they sat together without the barrier of walls either around or between them. What had started out as one of the most miserable days of his life was once again, because of Alec Tarley, turning into a beautiful moment worth remembering, despite the fact that ruminating on such beauty caused tears to well in his eyes.

If this was all they had, then it would be enough for Ian.

He just worried, in all the softest parts of his heart, that it wouldn't do for Tarley.

That Tarley deserved more than what loving him would condemn him to.

"It won't last, you know," Ian said, as a tear tracked down his cheek.

Beside him, Tarley stopped rocking. "Good and natural things rarely do."

Tarley sat his teacup aside and used the round of his knuckle to wipe away the dampness that Ian was too proud to draw further attention to. Tarley then scooted his chair closer, gathered Ian's hand in his own, and smiled. "The fact that the milk for your tea will eventually spoil doesn't stop you from enjoying it now, right? While it's still good?"

Ian looked at the joining of their hands without being able to unsee how his wrought and wrinkled fingers contrasted with Tarley's strong ones—or just how wonderful it was, despite.

"Quite right," Ian answered, his own smile flickering back to a reluctant life.

Satisfied, Tarley nodded, though did not relinquish his grip on Ian's hand, while their attentions turned back to the garden and the world beyond what would await them whenever the phone finally did ring.

"Until then...whatever shall we do?"

Mockingbirds sang, and the wind whispered through the hollow, as the creak of rocking chairs gliding on old wooden deck boards signaled the season's change. And for the first time in almost three decades, Ian Devonshire's hand was warmed by something other than a cup of tea.

Acknowledgements

The concept of this book came to me when I challenged myself to write a novella-length piece for an anthology centered on older characters. Almost immediately, Ian's voice began speaking to me; and little did I know how profoundly this love story would evolve. It became evident that Ian and I had a lot more in common than I first realized, and while I initially tried to deny those similarities because it felt too painful to write into, I also knew that this wasn't just a story I wanted to tell, it was one I knew I needed to.

This letter of gratitude would be longer than the novella if I tried to individually commend each and every person who has assisted in this publication. From volunteering to put eyes on the first drafts, to helping me with print sizes and formats, *An Appreciation of Cats* has been a labor of love that has certainly taken a village. If you have ever been kind enough to answer a question, spare a minute to check out my drafts, or have even shared a post about this novella to your social media, my eternal gratitude is extended to you. With that being said, I did want to mention a few individuals expressly:

To the CWC, thank you for all your inspiration, guidance and good humor. Y'all are the real MVPs.

Thank you to Lavender, who helped me ensure an accurate portrayal of the veterinary profession.

Thank you to Blake and Sam, who saw some of the earliest drafts, and have become great friends of mine, and champions of the piece ever since.

Thank you to Ashley and Madison, whose thoughtful feedback helped shape the story and whose unwavering support I have been so touched by.

Thank you to Autumn, Jem, and Sarah for triple-checking my British-isms; and to Ben for reminding me that I should be specific with my tea.

Thank you to Puhala, Steve and Tanner for being outstanding sensitivity readers.

Thank you, Val, for crafting the sweetest illustrations that have become so integral to this publication.

Thank you, Isaiah, for being my number one fan.

Thank you, Kell, for encouraging me to listen to my characters and to let the story be what it needed to be, no matter where it took me.

Thank you, Orlando, for the Write Hard class, which I was attending while writing the bulk of this story. I learned so much about writing past my own emotional barriers, and I'm confident that without that course, this novella wouldn't be what it is.

Thank you, Kacie, for bringing these characters to life with your artistic prowess. All of the time we spent discussing them, their features and mannerisms was well worth it in making them as real as something can be in a 2D space.

Thank you, Melissa. I would be very hard pressed to trust my book baby with anyone else—and I am extremely glad to have found an editor that is so knowledgeable and thorough, but also completely respects, understands, and encourages my unique voice.

Thank you to Ian and Tarley, who have irrevocably changed my life forever.

Thank you to my husband, who has been the unwavering support beam of my entire life. Thank you for always being up to listen to my next grand idea, for reading everything first, and for being completely honest with me when things aren't working. Without you, and your belief in my writing, you wouldn't have an author for a wife. I love you.

And thank you, reader, for picking up this book, and for giving a fledgling author a chance. It is my greatest honor to share these words with you, and I am hopeful to be able to do so for many years to come.

Keep reading, and I'll keep writing.

About the Author

Des DeVivo is a queer writer of queer stories that transmute pain into beauty. Born and raised in small-town Ohio, they now reside in Los Angeles with their husband and three cats.

The couple are college sweethearts, who were married on October 31st. This is where Des claims they've got the credentials for writing stories with HEAs, because she is married to a real life German Shepard book boyfriend.

When they aren't writing or at their day job, Des is reading, running, and visiting the beach as much as she can. Des has completed two marathons and plans to continue to train for more, with a goal of running in different cities around the world. She is also a survivor of melanoma—an experience that has made them want to cherish their health, and to live their life to the fullest—which is when they made the push to become a published author.

An Appreciation of Cats is their debut publication.

To learn more about Des DeVivo, future publications, and events, please scan the QR code or visit https://desdevivo.com